Room on the Broom

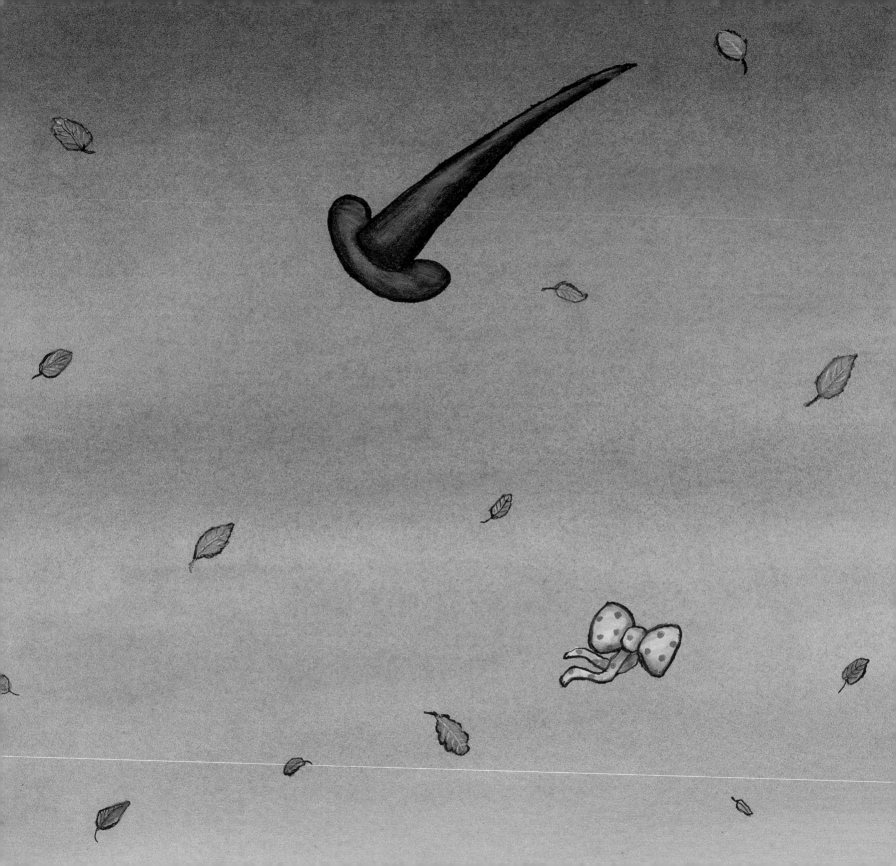

For Natasha, Sabrina and Jasmine—J.D.

ISBN 0-439-44412-8

Text copyright © 2001 by Julia Donaldson.
Pictures copyright © 2001 by Axel Scheffler. All rights reserved.
Published by Scholastic Inc., 557 Broadway, New York, NY 10012,
by arrangement with Dial Books for Young Readers,
a member of Penguin Putnam Inc. SCHOLASTIC and associated logos are
trademarks and/or registered trademarks of Scholastic Inc.

12 11 10 9 8 7 6 5 4 3 2 1   3 4 5 6 7/0

Printed in the U.S.A.   08

First Scholastic printing, October 2002

Room on the Broom

by Julia Donaldson

pictures by Axel Scheffler

SCHOLASTIC INC.

New York Toronto London Auckland Sydney
Mexico City New Delhi Hong Kong Buenos Aires

The witch had a cat
    and a hat that was black,
And long ginger hair
    in a braid down her back.
How the cat purred
    and how the witch grinned,
As they sat on their broomstick
    and flew through the wind.

But how the witch wailed
    and how the cat spat,
When the wind blew so wildly,
    it blew off the hat.

"Down!" cried the witch,
and they flew to the ground.
They searched for the hat,
but no hat could be found.

Then out of the bushes
on thundering paws
There bounded a dog
with the hat in his jaws.

He dropped it politely,
   then eagerly said
(As the witch pulled the hat
   firmly down on her head),
   "I am a dog, as keen as can be.
   Is there room on the broom
   for a dog like me?"

"Yes!" cried the witch,
   and the dog clambered on.
The witch tapped the broomstick and
   whoosh! they were gone.

Over the fields and the
　　forests they flew.
The dog wagged his tail
　　and the stormy wind blew.
The witch laughed out loud
　　and held on to her hat,
But away blew the bow
　　from her braid—just like that!

Then out from a tree,
    with an ear-splitting shriek,
There flapped a green bird
    with the bow in her beak.
She dropped it politely
    and bent her head low,

"Down!" cried the witch,
    and they flew to the ground.
They searched for the bow,
    but no bow could be found.

Then she filled up her cauldron
and said with a grin,
"Find something, everyone,
throw something in!"
So the frog found a lily,
the cat found a cone,
The bird found a twig,
and the dog found a bone.

They threw them all in
and the witch stirred them well,
And while she was stirring,
she muttered a spell.
"Iggety, ziggety, zaggety, ZOOM!"

Then out rose . . .

A TRULY
MAGNIFICENT BROOM!

With seats for the witch
    and the cat and the dog,
A nest for the bird and
    a pool for the frog.

"Yes!" cried the witch,
    and they all clambered on.
The witch tapped the broomstick and
    whoosh! they were gone.